D1172167

ABOUT THE AUTHORS

Joanne Meier, PhD, has worked as an elementary school teacher, university professor, and researcher. She earned her BA in early childhood education from the University of South Carolina, and her MEd and PhD in education from the University of Virginia. She currently works as a literacy consultant for schools and private organizations. Joanne lives in Virginia with her husband Eric, daughters Kella and Erin, two cats, and a gerbil.

Cecilia Minden, PhD, is the former director of the Language and Literacy Program at the Harvard Graduate School of Education. She is now a reading consultant for school and library publications. She earned her PhD in reading education from the University of Virginia. Cecilia and her husband, Dave Cupp, live outside Chapel Hill, North Carolina. They enjoy sharing their love of reading with their grandchildren, Chelsea and Qadir.

ABOUT THE ILLUSTRATOR

Bob Ostrom has been illustrating children's books for nearly twenty years. A graduate of the New England School of Art & Design at Suffolk University, Bob has worked for such companies as Disney, Nickelodeon, and Cartoon Network. He lives in North Carolina with his wife Melissa and three children, Will, Charlie, and Mae.

ABOUT THE SERIES CREATOR

Herbie J. Thorpe had long envisioned a beginning-readers' series about a fun, energetic bear with a big imagination. Herbie is a book lover and an avid supporter of libraries and the role they play in fostering the love of reading. He consults with librarians and matches them with the perfect books for their students and patrons. He lives in Louisiana with his wife Misty and their daughter Carson.

The Child's World®

Published in the United States of America by The Child's World®
1980 Lookout Drive • Mankato, MN 56003-1705
800-599-READ • www.childsworld.com

Acknowledgments
The Child's World®: Mary Berendes, Publishing Director
The Design Lab: Kathleen Petelinsek, Design;
Gregory Lindholm, Page Production
Assistant colorist: Richard Carbajal

Library of Congress Cataloging-in-Publication Data
Meier, Joanne D.
  Best mates on the boat / written by Joanne Meier and Cecilia
Minden ; illustrated by Bob Ostrom.
    p. cm. – (Herbster readers)
  Summary: "In this simple story belonging to the fourth level of
Herbster Readers, young Herbie and his siblings have fun with
their imaginations while on their grandparents' boat"–Provided
by publisher.
  ISBN 978-1-60253-028-7 (library bound : alk. paper)
  [1. Boats and boating–Fiction. 2. Imagination–Fiction. 3. Bears–
Fiction.] I. Minden, Cecilia. II. Ostrom, Bob, ill. III. Title. IV. Series.
PZ7.M5148Be 2008
  [E]–dc22   2008002425

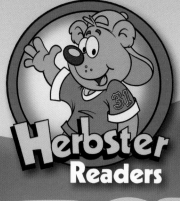

Herbster Readers

BEST MATES ON THE BOAT

Written by Joanne Meier and Cecilia Minden • Illustrated by Bob Ostrom
Created by Herbie J. Thorpe

"Let's go, Pappy!" Herbie shouted.
Herbie couldn't wait to go on the boat.

Pappy and Nana live on Lake Ann.
They have a boat.

During the summer, Herbie's family goes
to the lake for weekends. It is lots of fun!

Herbie waited on the dock. Everyone got ready.

Mom and Dad gathered sunscreen and towels.
Hannah grabbed her book and a bottle of water.
Hank carried a green pool noodle.

Nana brought a cooler full of snacks and drinks.

"Does everyone have their life jacket on?" asked Pappy.

"It looks like we're ready," said Nana.

The weather was perfect. There was a breeze. The sun was shining. It was going to be a great day!

Pappy got behind the wheel of the boat.
"Anchors aweigh!" shouted Herbie.
Pappy smiled. Herbie took his seat.

Pappy pushed the boat lever forward. The boat moved away from the dock. It slowly sped up.

"Want to drive the boat, Herbie?" asked Pappy.
Pappy always let Herbie drive.

Herbie sat with Pappy. He held the steering wheel with both hands.

There were some other boats on the water. They turned and zipped. This made the water choppy.

Pappy's boat glided up and down through the waves.

"Herbie, let's steer closer to shore," said Pappy.
"Aye, Captain!" said Herbie in his best pirate's voice.

"I see another ship off the bow. Let's make room for those landlubbers," Herbie said.

"What is Herbie talking about?" asked Hannah.

Pappy winked at Hannah.

"First Mate Herbie sees another boat," whispered Pappy. "It's in front of us."

Hannah decided to join the fun.
"Ahoy there, mate," Hannah said. "We've
got ourselves quite a wind today."

"Aye, these high seas are mighty rough," said Herbie.

"I hear high winds can bring out sea monsters,"
said Pappy. Just then, Hannah jumped as a
slimy green nose curled around her head.

Hank giggled. He had played a trick on Hannah with the green pool noodle!

"Clear the deck, mates. I see land," Herbie said.
"Aye, Captain," said Hannah.

Herbie steered the boat toward their favorite swimming spot.

"Land ho!" shouted Herbie.

Herbie and Pappy steered the boat into a cove. They slowed the boat down. The engine hummed. Dad lowered the anchor into the water.

"Well done, mate," said Pappy
as he patted Herbie's back.

"Thanks, Captain," said Herbie. "I couldn't have done it without my best mates on board."

Everyone just smiled.